It was time to line
up. Babe ran to get
in line.

"I am big," said Babe.
"It is time I got to line
up."

A man came up to Babe.
The man had Babe sit.

Babe was sad.

A dog ran up to Babe.

The dog had a cute hat.

"Take the hat," said
the dog.
"It is mine."

"Get in line," said the
dog.
"I can ride on top."

The dog got on Babe
and Babe ran to get
in line.

Babe and the dog
came to a tub.
"Get up on the tub,"
said the dog.

Babe got up on the tub.
"Sit up," said the dog.

Babe sat up.
The dog sat on Babe.

10

The man gave Babe a
pole.
"Wave the pole," said
the dog.

Babe and the dog got
in line.
As they rode in line,
Babe waved the pole.

Babe went up to a man.
The man gave Babe a
cone.
His wife gave the dog
a rose.

Babe ate the cone.
The dog gave Babe
the rose.

Babe sat up.
The dog sat up.

Babe made a big hit.